LOOK AT ME!

A Book of Occupations

By Dorothy Marcic Hai ✳ *Illustrated by* Eugenie

To Roxanne, who started it all

A GOLDEN BOOK · NEW YORK
Western Publishing Company, Inc., Racine, Wisconsin 53404

Look at me!
I'm an airplane pilot.

When I look out the windshield
of my airplane, I see the blue sky
and white clouds.

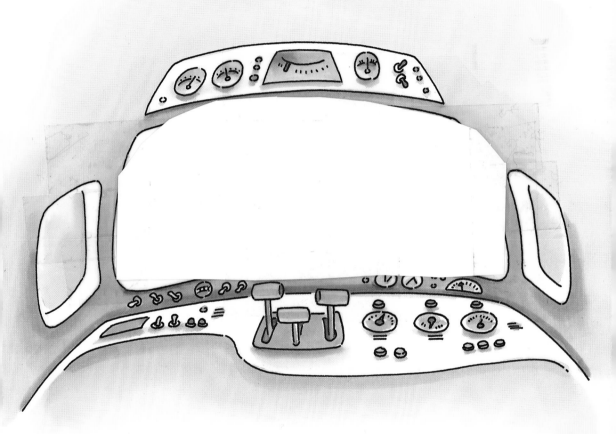

When I look through my binoculars,
I can see a boat that is far away.

Far below are hills and lakes and trees.

Look at me!
I'm a sailor.

The other boats are sailing
closer to the shore.

Look at me!
I'm a schoolteacher.

When I open the door to the classroom,
I see the children inside.

Open the door.

The children are busy working.

Open the door again and see me.

Look at me!
I'm a forest ranger.

When I look out my tower,
I see trees…

...birds, and many forest animals.

Look at me!
I'm a farmer.

Look at me!
I'm a bus driver.

When I look out the windshield
of my bus, I see cars, trucks,
and other buses.

I drive carefully on the busy, busy road.